My cat
and
A rainy day

Nelson

My cat

This is my cat.
My cat is fat.

My cat is getting fatter
and fatter.

One day my cat hid.
We looked under the bed.
She was not there.

We looked under the table.
She was not there.

We looked in the shed.

She was not there.

We called and called but
she did not come.

We looked in my box.
What did we see.
Six little kittens,
all for me.

A rainy day

It is wet.
I can't go out to play.

Mum says,
Here is a big box.

Look. My box is a . . . . **train.**
Toot, toot. I am going in a tunnel.

Look. My box is a . . . . **boat.**
Chug, chug. I am on the sea.

Look. My box is a . . . . **jet.**
Eeeaaawww. I can fly in the sky.

Look. My box is a . . . . **rocket.**
5, 4, 3, 2, 1, zero.
I am going to the moon.

Here is my Dad.
What did you do today,
said Dad.

I went in a train.

I went in a boat.

I went in a jet.

I went in a . . . . **rocket.**

Buster's Big Surprise

Little Red Robin

📖SCHOLASTIC

Scholastic Children's Books
An imprint of Scholastic Ltd.
Euston House, 24 Eversholt Street
London, NW1 1DB, UK
Registered office: Westfield Road, Southam, Warwickshire, CV47 0RA
SCHOLASTIC and associated logos are trademarks and/or registered
trademarks of Scholastic Inc.

First published in the UK in 2003 by Scholastic Ltd
This edition published in 2014 by Scholastic Ltd

Text copyright © Kaye Umansky, 2003
Illustrations © Mark Beech, 2014

The rights of Kaye Umansky and Mark Beech
to be identified as the author and illustrator of
this work have been asserted by them.

ISBN 978 1407 14278 4

A CIP catalogue record for this book is available from the British Library

Printed in China.

1 3 5 7 9 10 8 6 4 2

www.scholastic.co.uk/zone

Chapter One

Buster Gutt, the pirate chief, leaned on the ship's rail, scratching Bowzer's ear and thinking dark thoughts about his arch-enemy, Admiral Ainsley Goldglove.

Buster was the biggest, baddest pirate who ever sailed the seven seas. He and his crew had a terrible reputation. They bristled with pistols and cutlasses and would do anything for treasure.

Buster's ship was called *The Bad Joke* – people trembled whenever they saw it coming.

the bad joke

The only person who didn't tremble was
Admiral Ainsley Goldglove, of the *HMS Glorious*.
The admiral's noble chest dripped with medals
for catching pirates. He always wore a gold glove
on his left hand, just for show. Buster hated him.

"Catch me, would he?" he growled to Bowzer.

"Ha! We'll see about that!" Bowzer bared his
teeth in agreement.

Their little talk was suddenly interrupted by the crew, who had some very bad news indeed.

"What?" snarled Buster. "No food? 'Ow come?"

One-Eyed Ed, the lookout, shrugged and rolled his eye. Threefingers Jake, the bosun, nudged Jimmy Maggot, the cook, who stepped forward.

"We ate it all, Captain," he explained.

"But what 'appened to the ship's biscuits?" Buster growled.

"Weevils got 'em," said Jimmy Maggot.

"What about last week's sea pie?" snarled Buster.

"Went mouldy," sighed Jimmy Maggot. "I gave it to Bowzer. And that's not all. We're out of fresh water too."

"Sharksbum!" bellowed Buster. "We be scuppered!"
(In pirate speak, that means, "Oh, bother. We're
finished.")

"Not quite, Captain," said Threefingers Jake,
unrolling a chart. "There's land ahead, accordin'
to this. See? Allspice Island. Put your glass eye in,
Ed, and climb the rigging. See if you can spot it."

"No need!" croaked Timothy Tiddlefish, the cabin boy, who always had a cold. He wiped his nose on his sleeve and pointed across the water to a fast-approaching hump covered with trees. "There it *is*, comin' – ahh-ahh-*achoo*!"

"'E's right," said Buster, grimly. "It is comin' at me. Fast, too. All 'ands on deck, *at the double*!"

The crew hopped to it. The anchor was lowered, the sails were furled and Crasher Jackson, the helmsman, was shaken awake and told to steer left a bit.

It was a close shave, but they avoided bumping
into Allspice Island – just.

"Phew!" said Buster. "That was close. Man
the boats, lads. We'll go ashore an' stock up on
hokey-cokey nuts an' them yeller carrots what
monkeys eat."

On the other side of the island,
the *HMS Glorious* had also
dropped anchor. Admiral Ainsley
Goldglove was in a bad mood.
He hadn't caught any
pirates lately, plus his
personal supply of
wine had run out.

"No wine? Well,
that won't do, will
it?" he said sharply
to the crew.

"Absolutely not,
Admiral," agreed
Crisply Pimpleby,
the first officer,
saluting smartly.

"Dear me, no," tutted Monty Marshmallow, the chef, and Seaman Scuttle, the deckhand. Private Derek Plankton (nothing special) kept quiet. He just carried on dusting.

"Well, what are you waiting for?" cried the Admiral. "Allspice Island's just off the port bow. There are sure to be grapes. Grapes make wine, don't they? You can trample them. Launch the boats without delay." The admiral waved his gold glove and everyone jumped to it. Even Private Derek Plankton dusted a bit harder.

Chapter Two

Allspice Island turned out to be not very nice at all. At least, it wasn't on the side where Buster and his crew landed. The beach was full of rocks and smelly seaweed.

"Yuck!" moaned Crasher Jackson. "Pongy!"

"Is it?" sniffed Timothy Tiddlefish, who could never smell a thing.

It wasn't much better inland either. There were no coconuts or bananas to be seen. Just stunted trees and a muddy swamp which looked like the perfect spot for crocodiles.

Buster sat on a rock and threw a stick for Bowzer as his crew went exploring.

"Here, Captain," said Jimmy Maggot, coming back from the swamp with the crew at his heels and a very small cup of water in his hands. "Try this. I strained it through me scarf sixteen times."

Just then, Timothy Tiddlefish felt another
sneeze coming on. He tried to hold it back, but it was
no use. *"Rrrrrrraaachooo!"*

He sneezed right into the cup! It was a direct hit.

"You *twit*, Tiddlefish!" bellowed Buster. "Get out o' my sight! An' take yer nose with you! It should be able to keep up. It runs enough."

Snuffling, Timothy Tiddlefish wandered away, past the swamp and into the dark jungle.

On the other side of Allspice Island, it was a very different story. Little waves rippled on a stretch of golden sand. There were trees laden with bananas and coconuts. Rock pools teemed with fish and a freshwater spring bubbled brightly.

Admiral Ainsley Goldglove relaxed in the shade of a palm tree.

"Found any grapes yet, Pimpleby?" he enquired.

"Afraid not, Admiral," said Crisply Pimpleby, clicking his heels. "But Seaman Scuttle's found a lemon tree and there's certainly no shortage of fish."

"Hmm," said the admiral. "In that case, I think a barbecue is called for.

Grilled swordfish with sliced lemon, followed by banana trifle. See to it."

"Right away, sir," cried Pimpleby. "Marshmallow! Start slicing lemons. Plankton! Stop dusting that rock and start gathering sticks for the barbecue!"

Duster in hand, Private Derek Plankton trudged off.

Some time later, in the middle of the island, Timothy Tiddlefish and Private Derek Plankton bumped into each other. They were very surprised.

"Hello," said Private Derek Plankton, warily. "What are you doing here?"

"Sneezing," sighed Timothy. "*Atishoo!*"

"I'm Private Derek Plankton," said Private Derek Plankton.

They stared at each other for a bit.

"What are *you* doing here?" asked Timothy.

"Getting sticks for Admiral Goldglove's barbecue."

"*Admiral Goldglove?*" gasped Timothy. "*Here?*
On this island?"

"Yes. Usually I just do the dusting, but – hey!
Where are you going?"

There was no reply, apart from faraway
crashing noises and a distant sneeze.

Chapter Three

"*Goldglove?*" snarled Buster Gutt. "'Ere? On this island?"

"Yes!" said Timothy, excitedly. "He's having a barb-*achoo*! Am I still in trouble?"

"Nope," said Buster. "You done good, Tiddlefish. Bosun! Round up the crew."

"Why?" asked Timothy, eagerly. "What are we going to do?"

"Sneak up on 'em, o' course," said Buster. "Soon as it's dark. We'll sneak up, give 'em a bashin', tie 'em up an' eat their barbecue. Then we'll nick their boats an' row out to their ship and pinch their stuff."

"Attaboy, Captain!" cheered Threefingers Jake.

"Atta-*atishoo*!" agreed Timothy Tiddlefish.

The moon was high when Buster Gutt and his
crew crept through the undergrowth and peered
down at the beach, where Admiral Ainsley
Goldglove and his crew were having their barbecue.
The admiral sat at a folding table, dabbing his
lips with a napkin.

"Look at 'im, with 'is fancy ways!" growled
Buster. "I'll give 'im gold glove! Come on, let's
get 'em!"

And with one accord, they rose and burst from
the trees, yelling at the tops of their voices.

It should have worked. After all, Admiral
Ainsley Goldglove's crew weren't expecting to be
attacked.

They were stuffed with fish and bananas and didn't even have their weapons to hand.

What they did have, though, were heaped, slippery piles of bananas skins and an awful lot of coconuts!

Buster's crew came racing down the beach, waving their fearsome cutlasses and shouting (and sneezing) in a threatening manner.

Admiral Ainsley Goldglove calmly folded his napkin as he watched them approach.

"Dear me," he said. "It seems that we have uninvited guests. Captain Gutt and his crew, no less. You know the drill, men. Fire at will." And he waved his gold-gloved hand.

Seconds later, the air was full of flying coconuts.

There were pained cries as piratical skulls connected with coconuts, and piratical feet skidded on banana skins.

As each pirate hit the ground, he was pounced
on by Crisply Pimpleby and tied up with lengths
of vine. Even Bowzer had his paws trussed.

Buster was the last to go
down. He was still waving his
cutlass and howling threats
when a well-aimed coconut
hit his ear, landing him in a
pile of slippery banana skins.

After slithering several metres and swallowing
a lot of sand, he, too, was trussed up with vines.

"So, Gutt," said Admiral Ainsley Goldglove, strolling up. "We meet at last. You've given me the slip once too often. What have you got to say for yourself, eh?"

"Blurk!" muttered Buster, spitting out sand.

"Quite," smirked the admiral. "Load the boats with supplies, men. Then we'll return and pick up this sorry lot and bring them to justice. Ho hum! Another medal for me."

"Hooray!" shouted the admiral's crew. Buster's crew said nothing.

Chapter Four

Meanwhile, what had become of Private Derek Plankton?

He was lost, that's what. First he wandered around looking for sticks. Then he did a bit of dusting.

Then he sat down on a log and hummed, watched by a tribe of parrots who seemed fascinated by his feather duster.

Hours later, he heard distant cries coming from somewhere off to the left. He gave a sigh, stood up and trudged off, dusting as he went.

He was very surprised at the scene that met his eyes when he finally reached the beach. Instead of a jolly barbecue, the beach was full of bound, groaning pirates.

Admiral Ainsley Goldglove and his crew were specks in the distance, rowing towards the *HMS Glorious* with their boats laden with supplies.

"Ooer," said Private Derek Plankton. "What happened?"

"There was a fight," groaned Timothy Tiddlefish. "We lost. Any chance of untying me? I really need to blow my nose."

"Do you think I should?" said Private Derek Plankton.

"Of course. We're friends, aren't we?"

"But suppose I get into trouble?"

"You won't," said Timothy, soothingly. "Look what a mess we're making of the beach. It'll be much tidier with us gone. You like things tidy, don't you?"

So Private Derek Plankton untied Timothy
Tiddlefish, and together they set about releasing
the rest of the crew.

Finally, everybody stood around rubbing their
sore heads and glaring out to sea.

"I'll get 'im, see if I don't!" snarled Buster,
shaking his fist.

"But not right now," said Threefingers Jake,
hastily.

"We should get back to *The Bad Joke*," said
One-Eyed Ed.

"We'll pick up some supplies on the way,"
suggested Jimmy Maggot. "I'll make a nice stew
to cheer you up, Captain."

"All right," said Buster, but he wasn't very happy.

Everyone was very grateful to Private Derek Plankton. Nobody actually said thank you, because that's not the pirate way. But Buster invited him to join the crew.

"No, thanks," said Private Derek Plankton. "I'd better stay here and clear up a bit before they come back."

That night, on board *The Bad Joke*, there was banana and coconut stew for supper, just as Jimmy Maggot had promised.

It made a change, but Buster didn't feel much like celebrating. He was too fed up about being beaten by Admiral Ainsley Goldglove.

"Think what it'll do to my reputation," he fretted.

"Oh no, Captain," chorused the crew.

"I'll get him yet," said Buster.

"Course you will, course you will."

"There's always a next time," pointed out Timothy Tiddlefish.

There was, too. But that's another story.

Contents

Members of the Safety Panel Working Party

Note on text:

Although written in the male gender, the terminology in this document refers to both men and women.

1. Introduction

The construction industry has an unenviable record in health and safety, which it must strive to put firmly into the past. This publication states the view of the Institution of Civil Engineers of the responsibilities of the professional civil engineer for health and safety.

Everyone concerned with construction has both a moral and a legal duty to take care, not only of his own health and safety, but also of the health and safety of others who might be put at risk by the individual's actions or failure to take action.

Historically, and under most forms of contract, the responsibility for the health and safety of those involved in, and affected by, the construction industry has rested with the contractors, and they have been deemed to have allowed for any consequent costs in their tenders. While the contractors and the subcontractors clearly have a continuing role to fulfil it is now clear that the focus should be on all those involved in the project.

The Construction (Design and Management) Regulations 1994 place duties on all members of project teams according to their functions within the project.

The industry comprises an aggregate of project teams whose members draw on the strengths of the organizations behind them. The project is designed and specified by the clients and professional advisers and physically produced by the contractors, suppliers and operatives. Such teams work together to produce complex and often outstanding results and, if they work more closely in the interests of the health and safety of all those they interface with, then they will improve that aspect enormously. This is not just a theory: in some parts of the industry where clients take a strong lead and sensibly provide the necessary resources, safety records are considerably better.

Professional responsibilities

The professional engineer, whether he is in the office or on site, must be fully conversant with his statutory obligations, the project-specific health and safety requirements, and the particular responsibilities relating to his own appointment.

The professional role for members of the Institution is set down in the following Rule for Professional Conduct[1]

- *Rule 1.* A member, in his responsibility to his Employer and to the profession, shall have regard to the public interest, particularly in matters of health and safety.

and more generally in

- *Rule 2.* A member shall discharge his professional responsibilities with integrity.

The professional engineer may encounter, from time to time, potentially disastrous situations which do not fall within established procedures. His duty of care coupled with the first Rule for Professional Conduct require him to react responsibly to such a situation. The Fellowship of Engineering has issued guidelines[2] to assist engineers in these circumstances.

Legally, professional engineers have responsibilities which include duties under statute, contract and in tort. Usually a contract will not repeat statutory duties; in any event it cannot override them.

All engineers should be aware that it is not possible to contract out of statutory health and safety obligations and that the tort of negligence covers a wide range of circumstances, which can coincide with a breach of contractual obligations.

In all circumstances the professional engineer should bear in mind that the Health and Safety Executive has estimated that 70% of construction site fatalities could have been prevented by effective management action.

Contractual responsibilities

Conditions of contract deal only with the civil liabilities of the parties to the contract. They do not relieve the Employer (client), the Engineer, the Contractor, subcontractors, or any employees or others working on a site of their duties under the Health and Safety at Work etc. Act 1974 or any other health and safety legislation.

Generally under the ICE Conditions of Contract (Fifth and Sixth Editions),[3] the ICE Conditions of Contract for Minor Works[4] and the ICE Design and Construct Conditions of Contract,[5] the Contractor is made responsible for the safety of all operations on site. In addition he can suspend work on safety grounds.

The ICE's New Engineering Contract[6] allows for particular health and safety requirements to be specified for each particular contract.

Legislation — an overview

There is a considerable body of legislation, recently influenced by EU Directives, governing health, safety and welfare in the construction industry. The legislation includes Acts of Parliament and Regulations dealing with both technical and management matters. Liability for breach of the duties under this legislation is criminal in nature. Conviction is likely to result in a fine or, possibly, imprisonment. While it is possible to insure against civil liability it is impossible to do so against criminal liability.

The Health and Safety at Work etc. Act 1974 provides a comprehensive framework to promote high standards of health and safety at work. Everyone is involved: managers, employees, the self-employed, and manufacturers and suppliers of equipment and materials. Where it is placed at risk by work activities, the health and safety of the public is also covered.

The Management of Health and Safety at Work

Regulations 1992 place detailed duties on employers and self-employed persons. They include such matters as

- risk assessment
- health and safety arrangements
- health and safety assistance
- co-operation and co-ordination
- capabilities and training.

The Construction (Design and Management) Regulations 1994 place specific duties on clients, designers and contractors to consider health and safety so that it is taken into account and then co-ordinated and managed effectively throughout all stages of a construction project — from conception, design and planning through to the execution of works on site, subsequent maintenance and repair, and eventual demolition. For many of the duty holders these regulations require a radical change in culture as well as training and education in the practical steps and procedures required.

2. Statutory requirements

The following is a digest of the main statutory requirements relating to the management of health and safety in the construction industry. It does not cover the legal requirements relating to prescriptive technical matters.

Health and Safety at Work etc. Act 1974

Members of the Institution and the organizations they represent have the following duties under the Health and Safety at Work etc. Act 1974 according to their relationship with others and/or their degree of control over places of work. Any combination of these duties may be held simultaneously.

Duty as employees at work

All employees have a duty

- to take reasonable care of their own health and safety and that of others who may be affected by what they do
- to co-operate with their employer or any other person who has a duty under any of the relevant statutory provisions so far as is necessary to ensure that their duty is complied with.

Members should carefully consider what this means in the contexts of their own positions and of those who are affected by what they do.

Duty as employers in relation to their employees

Employers (i.e. those who have contracts of employment with individuals) have a general duty to ensure, so far as is reasonably practicable, the health, safety and welfare of their employees. That general duty includes such matters as

- safe plant and systems of work
- the safe use, handling, storage and transport of articles and substances
- the provision of necessary information, instruction, training and supervision
- the maintenance of a safe place of work and the means of access and egress to and from that place
- a working environment which is safe and healthy and which includes adequate welfare facilities.

Employers with five or more employees must have a written policy on health and safety which must include details of the organization to be deployed and the arrangements to be implemented by that organization.

Duty as employers (or self-employed persons) to others who are not their employees

All employers and self-employed persons have a duty to conduct their undertakings to ensure that, so far as is reasonably practicable, others who are not their employees (including members of the public) are not exposed to risks to their health or safety as a result of that undertaking. This duty is very broad and members should carefully consider what it means in the context of their undertakings and the persons who are affected.

Duty as persons having control over places of work

Any person or organization who has control to any extent over any premises used for work by persons who are not their employees must ensure that they do everything reasonably practicable given their position to ensure that

- the premises themselves are safe
- all means of access to or egress from the premises are safe
- any plant or substances in or provided for use at the premises are safe and without risk to health.

Construction Regulations 1961 and 1966

The Construction Regulations 1961 and 1966, made under the Factories Act 1961, prescribe technical standards to be achieved in relation to

- general provisions such as excavations and demolition
- working places, which include scaffolding and means of access
- lifting operations, including the nature, testing, examination and use of cranes and other lifting gear
- health and welfare matters.

The duty to comply with these regulations rests with 'contractors and employers of workmen'.

Other regulations

There are a number of other regulations, covering such matters as noise, asbestos, lead and head protection, which must be complied with. The duty to comply with them generally rests with the employer. Duties under these regulations exist simultaneously with duties under the Health and Safety at Work etc. Act 1974 and under both the Management of Health and Safety at Work Regulations 1992 and the Construction (Design and Management) Regulations 1994 which cover the management of health and safety at work in the construction industry.

3. Main requirements of the Management of Health and Safety at Work Regulations 1992

Risk assessment

All employers and self-employed persons are required

- to assess the risks to both their own employees and others arising out of their undertakings
- then to identify the measures they need to take to comply with the relevant statutory provisions.

Such assessments must be reviewed as necessary, and where there are five or more employees significant findings must be recorded.

Health and safety arrangements

Every employer must make arrangements for the effective planning, organization, control, monitoring and review of the measures previously established as necessary and record the arrangements if five or more people are employed. This may not be a particularly onerous exercise if the risks are well known and the means of dealing with them are well established. In other circumstances significant research may be necessary.

Health and safety assistance

Every employer must have access to one or more persons to assist him to carry out the measures identified. The quantity and quality of that assistance will depend on the nature of the undertaking. The traditional role of the safety officer in contracting organizations may become a wider ranging professional role and many design/specifying organizations will need their own specialists in this field. Many organizations will also need access to specialist engineering and scientific skills in order to deal with complex health and safety problems.

Co-operation and co-ordination

All employers sharing a work place must co-operate with each other and share information in the interests of health and safety. This is particularly relevant to the construction industry. Specific requirements for doing this are in the Construction (Design and Management) Regulations 1994.

Capabilities and training

Employers must ensure that their employees are capable of undertaking the health and safety responsibilities appropriate to their jobs and have received adequate health and safety training. This applies at all levels, including top management. It is essential on recruitment or transfer to a site because statistics show that a high proportion of accidents happen to persons during their first few days on a particular site.

Control of risks

There are a number of ways of dealing with risks and it is a requirement of the Approved Code of Practice[7] associated with these regulations that a hierarchical approach be adopted. Each step must be exhausted so far as is reasonably practicable, and if significant risk remains then the next step must be applied.

The following approaches should be executed in sequence.

- *Elimination.* It is often possible to eliminate risks by substitution or by simply not doing something which is not really necessary. For example, large-diameter augered piles may be marginally the best foundation engineering solution to a large structure to be built on contaminated land. However, the process will bring hazardous materials to the surface and expose workers and others to foreseeable risks. The alternative of driven piles eliminates that risk and, although it may be more expensive, it could be a reasonably practicable way forward.

- *Reduction.* There are some areas where it is not possible to eliminate risks without compromising other essential features of a project, but if it is possible to reduce them this must be done.
- *Collective protection.* Collective protection which does not rely on discipline or spasmodic action by individuals for its effectiveness must be provided. For example, acoustic shielding of a noisy compressor or — better still — its replacement by a less noisy machine should be used wherever possible in preference to hearing protection being provided.
- *Organizational controls.* Organizational controls are special rules or procedures. The permit to work system is the most common. Such procedures necessarily rely for their effectiveness on someone taking specific action and therefore should be relied on only if there is no reasonably practicable alternative. The role of the temporary works co-ordinator is an example of an organizational control.
- *Personal protection.* Personal protection will inevitably be required, depending on the nature of the work and the hazards involved, because it is not practicable to reduce all risks in construction to negligible levels. Items of personal protection should be avoided as a primary means of controlling risk. In order to comply with the Construction (Head Protection) Regulations 1989, the provision of head protection is necessary on

all construction sites unless those in control of a site decide that there is no risk of head injury. Similarly, in order to comply with the Personal Protective Equipment Regulations 1992, all other forms of personal protective equipment must be provided where a risk exists.

4. Components of risk

Before embarking on any risk assessment it is essential to have a clear understanding of hazard and risk.

- *Hazard* is something with the potential for harm.
- *Risk* expresses the likelihood that the harm from a particular hazard is realized and the consequences for the persons exposed to the risk.

Techniques of hazard identification and risk assessment, management and control are available.
A suitable and sufficient risk assessment should

- identify in a structured manner the significant risks arising out of work
- enable the employer or the self-employed person to identify and prioritize the measures that are needed to comply with the law — these measures should be appropriate to the nature of the work being undertaken.

For further guidance see the Management of Health and Safety at Work Regulations 1992 and Approved Code of Practice.

5. Main requirements of the Construction (Design and Management) Regulations 1994

The following is a digest, based on Health and Safety Executive guidance,[8] of the Construction (Design and Management) Regulations 1994. Those requiring a comprehensive understanding should study the full text of the Regulations and the Approved Code of Practice.[7] The Regulations contain exemptions for certain minor works, but demolition work of any nature is never exempted.

Duties of clients

It is recognized that many clients have little or no knowledge of industry practices and cannot be expected to make a detailed technical contribution to control health and safety risks. However, the ultimate source of the resources necessary to complete a project with the minimum of risk to health and safety is the client. The client's duties include

- to appoint a planning supervisor in respect of the project
- to appoint a principal contractor in respect of the project
- to ensure that those he appoints have the competence to perform their functions and will allocate adequate resources for the purpose
- to ensure that the construction phase does not start until a health and safety plan has been prepared.

The client may appoint members of his own staff or departments within his own organization — provided they are competent — to carry out these duties. The principal contractor must be a contractor, i.e. a person who undertakes or manages construction work.

Duties of planning supervisor

The planning supervisor's duties include

- to ensure that the design complies with the Regulations
- to ensure co-operation between designers
- to be in a position to advise the client or any contractor on the competence of persons appointed to design or manage construction work
- to be in a position to advise clients on the adequacy of resources allocated by others
- to ensure that a health and safety file is prepared and eventually given to the client
- to ensure that a health and safety plan is prepared for the project containing the information required by the Regulations, in time for it to be provided to any contractor before arrangements are made for him to carry out the work (this will usually mean providing the plan as part of the tender documentation).

Duties of designers

Many of the risks arising from construction can be greatly reduced, if not eliminated, if due consideration is given to them at the appropriate stage in the design process and if information is given about the measures necessary to control the residual risks in the design.

The designer's duties[8] are, so far as is reasonably practicable

- to alert clients to their duties
- to consider during the development of designs the hazards and risks which may arise to those constructing and maintaining the structure
- to design to avoid risks to health and safety as far as is reasonably practicable
- to reduce risks at source if avoidance is not possible

- to consider measures which will protect all workers if neither avoidance nor reduction to a safe level is possible
- to ensure that the design includes adequate information on health and safety
- to pass this information on to the planning supervisor so that it can be included in the health and safety plan, and to ensure that it is given on drawings or in specifications and so on
- to co-operate with the planning supervisor and, where necessary, other designers involved in the project.

Duties and powers of principal contractor

The principal contractor has to take over and develop the health and safety plan and co-ordinate the activities of all contractors so that they comply with health and safety law.[8]
  The principal contractor's key duties are

- to develop and implement the health and safety plan
- where the work is subcontracted, to arrange for competent and adequately resourced contractors to carry it out
- to ensure the co-ordination and co-operation of contractors
- to obtain from contractors the main findings of their risk assessments and details of how they intend to carry out high-risk operations
- to ensure that contractors have information about risks on site
- to ensure that workers on site have been given adequate training
- to ensure that contractors and workers comply with any site rules which may have been set out in the health and safety plan
- to monitor health and safety performance

- to ensure that all workers are properly informed and consulted
- to make sure only authorized people are allowed on to the site
- to pass information to the planning supervisor for the health and safety file.

The principal contractor may

- give reasonable directions to any contractor
- include in the health and safety plan rules for the management of the work.

Duties of and prohibitions on contractors

Every contractor must

- provide information for the health and safety plan about risks to health and safety arising from their work and steps they will take to control and manage the risks
- manage their work so that they comply with rules in the health and safety plan and co-operate with the principal contractor
- provide information for the health and safety file, and information about injuries, dangerous occurrences and ill health
- provide information to their employees.

The self-employed also have these duties when they act as contractors.

Competence and resources of planning supervisor, designers and contractors

Persons making appointments must be satisfied that persons appointed

- are competent to deal with the health and safety

aspects of the project

- have allocated adequate resources.

There must be a structured procedure which concludes that those appointed are competent and have allocated adequate resources.

6. Conclusions

It is clear that, in whatever capacity they work in the construction industry, members of the Institution have a duty of care and are accountable for making their contribution to preserving the health and safety of anyone who may be affected by their work arising from

- statutory duties
- contractual commitments
- professional duties.

As a result individuals must

- organize themselves personally to meet their responsibilities
- engage in a programme of continuous professional development to ensure that they keep themselves informed on health and safety
- include health and safety in all job descriptions and similar documents.

and organizations must

- understand that health and safety is an integral part of good management
- allocate high priority and adequate resources to health and safety matters.

References

1. Institution of Civil Engineers. In *Royal Charter, By-laws, Regulations and Rules*. ICE, London, 1992.
2. Fellowship of Engineering. *Preventing disasters*. FEng, London, 1991.
3. Institution of Civil Engineers *et al*. *ICE Conditions of Contract*. Thomas Telford, London, fifth edition 1986, sixth edition 1991.
4. Institution of Civil Engineers *et al*. *ICE Conditions of Contract for Minor Works*, second edition. Thomas Telford, London, 1995.
5. Institution of Civil Engineers *et al*. *ICE Design and Contract Conditions of Contract*. Thomas Telford, London, 1992.
6. Institution of Civil Engineers. *The New Engineering Contract*. Thomas Telford, London, 1993.
7. Health and Safety Executive. *Managing construction for health and safety*. Approved code of practice for the CDM Regulations. HSE Books, London, 1995.
8. Health and Safety Executive. *CDM Regulations — how the Regulations affect you*. HSE, London, 1995.

Bibliography

Anderson J. M. Managing safety in construction. *Proc. Instn Civ. Engrs* , 1992, **92**, 127–132.

Bielby S. *Site safety handbook for young professionals*. Construction Industry Research and Information Association, London, 1992.

Blockley D. *Engineering safety*. McGraw-Hill, London, 1992.

Anderson J. M. Construction (Design and Management) Regulations. *Proc. Instn Civ. Engrs*, 1994, **102**, May, 49–51.

Construction (General Provisions) Regulations 1961. SI 1961, No. 1580 as amended. HMSO, London, 1961.

Construction (Health and Welfare) Regulations 1996. SI 1966, No. 95 as amended. HMSO, London, 1966.

Construction (Lifting Operations) Regulations 1961. SI 1961, No. 1581 as amended. HMSO, London, 1961.

Construction (Working Places) Regulations 1966. SI 1966, No. 94 as amended. HMSO, London, 1966.

Total project management of construction safety, health and environment. European Construction Institute. Thomas Teford, London, 1992.

European Foundation for the Improvement of Living and Working Conditions. *From drawing board to building site.* HMSO, London, 1991.

Health and Safety Commission. *The health and safety system in Great Britain.* HSE Books, London, 1992.

Health and Safety Executive. *Blackspot construction — a study of 5 years' fatal accidents.* HMSO, London, 1988.

Health and Safety Executive. *Successful health and safety management.* HS(G)65. HSE Books, London, 1991.

Health and Safety Executive. *Cost of accidents at work.* HS(G)96. HSE Books, London, 1993.

Health and Safety Executive. *Essentials of health and safety at work.* HSE Books, London, 1994.

Health and Safety Executive. *The cost to the British economy of work accidents and work related ill health.* HSE Books, London, 1994.

Health and Safety Executive. *A guide to managing health and safety in construction.* HSE Books, London, 1995.

Health and Safety Executive. *Designing for health and safety in construction.* HSE Books, London, 1995.

Health and Safety Executive. *Health and safety for small construction sites.* HSE Books, London, 1995.

Joyce R. *The Construction (Design and Management) Regulations 1994 explained.* Thomas Telford, London, 1995.

Safety and health in the construction sector. Office for Official Publications of the European Community. Luxembourg, 1993.

Learning Resources
Centre